Enid Blyton

The Three
Naughty Children
and other stories

Illustrated by Eileen A. Soper

DRAGON
GRANADA PUBLISHING
London Toronto Sydney New York

Published by Granada Publishing Limited
in Dragon Books 1974
Reprinted 1978

ISBN 0 583 30179 7

First published by Macmillan & Co Ltd 1950

Granada Publishing Limited
Frogmore, St Albans, Herts AL2 2NF
and
3 Upper James Street, London W1R 4BP
1221 Avenue of the Americas, New York NY, 10020, USA
117 York Street, Sydney, NSW 2000, Australia
100 Skyway Avenue, Toronto, Ontario, Canada M9W 3A6
Trio City, Coventry Street, Johannesburg 2001, South Africa
CML Centre, Queen & Wyndham, Auckland 1, New Zealand

Made and printed in Great Britain by
Richard Clay (The Chaucer Press) Ltd
Bungay, Suffolk
Set in Monotype Baskerville

The Three Naughty Children
and other stories

Contents

THE THREE NAUGHTY CHILDREN

One day Queen Peronel's cook heard a knocking at her kitchen door. She opened it and saw a ragged pedlar there, his tray of goods in front of him.

'Can I sell you something?' said the pedlar. 'Red ribbons, silver thimbles, honey-chocolate, high-heeled shoes – I have them all here.'

'Nothing today, thank you,' said the cook. But the pedlar would not go.

'I am tired with walking many miles,' he said. 'Let me come in and rest a little. See, I will wipe my feet well on the mat so that I shall not dirty your clean kitchen floor.'

7

So the cook let him come in and sit down on her oldest chair for a little while. But when he had gone she missed three things, and flew to tell Queen Peronel.

'Oh, Your Highness!' she cried, bursting into the drawing-room where the Queen sat knitting a jersey. 'Oh, Your Highness, a pedlar has stolen your blue milk-jug, your little silver spoon and your wooden porridge plate! Oh, whatever shall I do!'

Now these three things were all full of magic and the Queen treasured them very much. The blue milk-jug had the power of pouring out perfectly fresh milk twice a day, which was very useful for the Queen's nurse, for she had two little princesses and a prince to look after

in the royal nursery. The silver spoon would make anyone hungry if he put it into his mouth, and this, too, was *very* useful if any of the royal children wouldn't eat a meal.

The wooden porridge plate could play a tune all the time that porridge was eaten from it, so the children loved it very much. Queen Peronel was dreadfully upset when she heard that all these things had been stolen.

'What was the pedlar like?' she asked. 'I will have him captured and put into prison.'

But alas, when the cook told her about the pedlar's looks, the Queen knew that he was no pedlar but a wizard who had dressed himself up to steal her treasures. She called the King and he really didn't know what to do.

'That wizard is too powerful for us to send to prison,' he said, shaking his head. 'He won't give us back those three things if we ask him nicely, for he will say he didn't steal them. I really do *not* know what to do.'

Now when the two little princesses and the prince heard how the wizard had stolen their milk-jug, porridge plate and spoon, they were very angry.

'Send a hundred soldiers to him, father, and capture him!' cried Roland, the little prince, standing straight and tall in front of the King.

'Don't be silly, my dear child,' said the King. 'He would turn them all into wolves and send them howling back here. You wouldn't like that, would you?'

'Well, father, send someone to steal all the things from *him*,' said Rosalind, the eldest child, throwing back her golden curls.

'You don't know what you are talking about,' said the King crossly. 'Go back to the nursery, all of you, and play at trains.'

They went back to the nursery, but they didn't play at trains. They sat in a corner and talked. Rosalind and Roland were very fierce about the stealing of their magic things. Then Roland suddenly thought of an idea.

'I say, Rosalind, what about dressing up as a wizard myself and going to call on the wizard who took away our things? Perhaps I could make him give them back. *I'm* not afraid of any old wizard!'

'I shall come, too,' said Rosalind, who liked to be in everything.

'And so shall I,' said Goldilocks, the youngest of them all.

'You're too little,' said Roland.

'I'm *not*!' said Goldilocks. 'I shall cry if you don't let me come.'

'All right, all right, you can come,' said Roland, 'but if you get turned into a worm or something, don't blame *me*!'

Then they made their plans, and very queer plans they were, too. They were all to slip out of bed that night and go downstairs, dressed, when nobody was about. Roland was to get his father's grandest cloak and feathered hat, and the two girls were to take with them a pair of bellows each, a box of fireworks from the

firework cupboard, and two watering-cans full of water. How strange!

They were most excited. They could hardly wait until the clock struck eleven and everyone else was in bed. Then they dressed and went downstairs. Soon Roland was wrapped in his father's wonderful gold and silver cloak, with big diamonds at the neck and round the hem. On his curly head he put his father's magnificent feathered hat, stuffed with a piece of paper inside to make it fit. Then, with their burden of bellows, fireworks and watering-cans, they set off to the wizard's little house on the hillside not far off.

It was all in darkness save for one light in the nearest window.

'He's still up,' said Roland. 'Good! Now, you two girls, you know what to do, don't you? As soon as you hear me shouting up the chimney, do your part. And if you make a mistake, Goldilocks, I'll pull your hair to-morrow, so there!'

'Help me to get the ladder out of the garden shed,' said Rosalind as they came near to the cottage. Roland and the two girls silently carried the ladder to the cottage and placed it softly against the roof. Then up went the two princesses, as quietly as cats. In half a minute they were sitting beside the chimney, their bellows, fireworks and watering-cans beside them.

It was time for Roland to do his part. He wrapped the big cloak around his shoulder and strode up to the door. He hammered on it with a stone he had picked up and made a tremendous noise. The wizard inside nearly jumped out of his skin.

'Now who can this be?' he wondered, getting up. 'Some great witch or enchanter, hammering like that on my door!'

He opened the door and Roland strode in, not a bit nervous.

'Good evening, wizard,' he said. 'I am Rilloby-Rimmony-Ru, the Enchanter from the moon. I have heard that you can do wondrous things. Show me some.'

The wizard looked at Roland's grand cloak and hat and thought he must indeed be a rich and great enchanter. He bowed low.

'I can command gold to come from the air, silver to come from the streams, and music from the stars,' he said.

'Pooh!' said Roland rudely, 'anyone can do that! Can you call the wind and make it do your bidding?'

'Great sir, no one can do that,' answered the wizard, mockingly.

'Ho, you mock at me, do you?' said Roland. He went to the chimney and shouted up it. 'Wind, come down to me and show this poor wizard how you obey my commands!'

At once Rosalind and Goldilocks began to work the bellows down the chimney, blowing great puffs of air down as they opened and

shut the bellows. The smoke from the fire was blown all over the room and the wizard began to cough. He looked frightened.

'Enough, enough!' he cried. 'You will smoke me out. Command the wind to stop blowing down my chimney.'

'Stop blowing, wind!' commanded Roland, shouting up the chimney. At once the two girls on the roof stopped working the bellows, and the smoke went up the chimney in the ordinary way.

'Wonderful, wonderful!' said the wizard, staring at Roland in amazement. 'I have never seen anyone make the wind his servant before.'

'That's nothing,' said Roland, grandly. 'I can command the rain, too.'

'Bid it come, then,' said the wizard, trembling. Roland shouted up the chimney. 'Rain, come at my bidding!' At once Rosalind and Goldilocks poured water down the chimney from their watering-cans and it hissed on the fire and spat out on the hearth. The wizard leapt back in alarm.

'Stop the rain!' he cried. 'It will put out my fire if it rushes down my chimney like that.'

Roland, who didn't at all want the fire to be put out, hastily shouted to the rain to stop, and the two little girls put their watering-cans down, giggling to hear the astonished cries of the wizard.

'Surely you can do no greater thing than these!' said the wizard to Roland.

'Well, I can command the thunder and lightning, too,' said Roland. 'Wait. I will call down some for you to see.'

Before the frightened wizard could stop

him Roland shouted up the chimney again. 'Thunder and lightning, come down here!'

Rosalind dropped a handful of fireworks down at once. They fell into the flames and exploded with an enormous bang, flashing brightly. The wizard yelled in alarm and ran into a corner. Rosalind dropped down some more fireworks, and two squibs hopped right out of the fire to the corner where the wizard was hiding.

'Oh, oh, the thunderstorm is coming after me!' he shouted. 'Take it away, great Enchanter, take it away!'

Roland badly wanted to laugh, but he dared not even smile. Another batch of fireworks fell down the chimney, and the wizard rushed away again and fell over a stool.

'Stop, thunder and lightning!' called Roland up the chimney. At once the girls stopped throwing down fireworks and there was peace and quiet in the room, save for the wizard's moans of fright.

'Am I not a powerful enchanter?' asked Roland, grandly. 'Would you not like to know my secrets?'

'Oh, Master, would you tell me them?' cried the wizard, delighted.

'I will write them down on a piece of paper for you,' said Roland, 'but you must not look at it until tomorrow morning. And now, what will you give me in return?'

'Sacks of gold, cart-loads of silver,' cried the grateful wizard.

'Pooh!' said Roland, scornfully. 'What's the use of those to me? I am richer than everyone in the world put together.'

'Then look round my humble dwelling and choose what takes your fancy,' said the wizard at once. 'See, I have strange things here – what would you like?'

Roland glanced round quickly and saw the blue milk-jug, the silver spoon and the porridge plate on a shelf.

'Hm!' he said, 'I don't see much that I like. Wait! Here is a pretty jug. I will take that in return for the secret of the wind. And here is a dainty silver spoon. That shall be my reward for the secret of the rain. Then what shall I

take for the secret of the thunder and lightning? Ah, here is a porridge plate I shall love to use. Wizard, I will take all these. Now see – here is an envelope. Inside you will find written the secret of the wind, the rain and the thunderstorm you have seen here tonight. Do not open it until tomorrow morning.'

He took the jug, the spoon and the porridge dish, and strode out of the door, the wizard bowing respectfully in front of him. Rosalind and Goldilocks had already climbed down the ladder and were waiting for him. They ran as fast as they could with all their watering-cans, bellows and other things, laughing till they cried when they thought of the clever tricks they had played.

And when the King and Queen heard of their prank they didn't know whether to scold or praise.

'You naughty, brave, rascally, daring scamps!' cried the Queen. 'Why, you might have been turned into frogs!'

As for the wizard, when he opened the envelope the next morning and saw what was written there, he was very puzzled indeed. For

this is what Roland had written: 'The secret of the wind is Bellows. The secret of the rain is Watering-cans. The secret of the thunder-storm is Fireworks. Ha! ha!'

And now the poor wizard is wandering all over the world trying to find someone wise and clever enough to tell him the meaning of the Bellows, the Watering-cans and the Fireworks, But nobody likes to!

THE TWO GOOD FAIRIES

David and Ruth lived in Primrose Cottage, and next door to them was Daffodil Cottage. An old man lived there, very fond of his garden, which was just a little piece like theirs.

One day the old man fell ill and had to go away to be nursed. David and Ruth peeped over the fence at his garden, which was full of daffodils and primroses.

'Old Mr. Reed will be sorry to leave his lovely daffodils before they are over,' said

Ruth. 'I wonder if his servant will look after his garden for him.'

'Mr. Reed was a cross old man,' said David. 'He used to frown if we shouted or made a noise.'

'And he hated to let us get a ball if it went over the fence,' said Ruth.

'He was never well,' said their mother. 'That is why he was cross. I expect if he had been well and strong like you he would have been jolly and good-tempered.'

The cottage next door was shut up and the hard-working little servant went back to her mother. There was no one to look after the garden, and as soon as the daffodils and primroses were over, the garden beds became full of weeds. The little lawn grew long and untidy, and thistles grew at the end of the garden.

'Isn't it a pity?' said Ruth, looking over the fence at the untidy garden. 'It used to be so nice in the summer-time, full of flowers. Now it is like a field!'

'I wonder when old Mr. Reed will come back,' said David.

'Mother says he is coming back in June,' said Ruth. 'Our garden will look lovely then, but his will be dreadful.'

'Let's go and buy our seeds tomorrow,' said David. 'We ought to be planting them now, you know, else our gardens will be late with their summer flowers.'

They emptied out their money-box and counted their money. They had plenty to buy seeds.

'I wish we had enough to buy a nice wheel-barrow, a new watering-can and a spade,' said David longingly. 'All our garden things are getting old. Shall we ask mother if she'll buy us some new ones?'

But mother said no. 'I can't afford it,' she

said. 'I am saving up to buy a new mangle, because mine is falling to bits. I'll see about your garden tools after I've bought a new mangle.'

'Oh dear,' said Ruth, 'that won't be for ages!'

The two children went off to the seedsman to buy their garden seeds. They bought candytuft, poppies, nasturtiums, virginia stock, love-in-a-mist and cornflowers – all the things that most children love to grow in their gardens. Then back they went to plant them.

They were very good little gardeners. They knew just how to get the beds ready, and how to shake the seed gently out of the packets so that not too much went into one place. They watered their seeds carefully and kept the weeds from the beds. Mother was quite proud of the way they kept their little gardens.

As they were planting their seeds Ruth had a good idea. She sat back on the grass and told it to David.

'I say, David, we've plenty of seeds this year, haven't we?' she said. 'Well, let's go and plant some next door in the little round bed just in front of the window where the old man sits every day. Even if his garden is in a dreadful state he will be able to see one nice flowery bed! It would be such a nice surprise for him!'

David thought it was a good idea. So when they had finished planting their seeds in their own little gardens the two children ran into the garden next door. Then they began to work very hard indeed.

The round bed was covered with weeds! So before any seeds were planted all the dandelions, buttercups and other weeds had to be dug up and taken away. Then the bed was

dug well over by David, and Ruth made the earth nice and fine.

Then they planted the seeds. In the middle they put cornflowers because they were nice and tall. Round them they put candytuft, with poppies here and there. In front they put love-in-a-mist with nasturtiums in between, and to edge the bed they planted seeds of the gay little virginia stock. They were so pleased when they had finished, for the bed looked very neat and tidy.

'There! That's finished,' said David. 'Now we've only got to come in and weed and water, and the bed will look lovely in the summer-time! How surprised old Mr. Reed will be!'

You should have seen how those seeds grew. It was wonderful. The children's gardens looked pretty enough, but the round bed next door was marvellous.

The cornflowers were the deepest of blues, and the candytuft was strong and sturdy. The virginia stock was full of buds.

'Old Mr. Reed is coming back tomorrow,' said Ruth in excitement. 'Won't he be surprised!'

He did come back – and he *was* surprised! The children peeped over the fence and saw him looking out of his window in the very greatest astonishment. He saw them and waved to them.

'Hallo, Ruth and David,' he said. 'Just look at that round bed! Isn't it a picture? I was so sad when I came back thinking that I wouldn't have any flowers in my garden this summer – and the first thing I saw was this lovely bed full of colour. Do *you* know who planted the seeds?'

David and Ruth didn't like to say that they had done it.

'Perhaps it was the fairies,' said Mr. Reed.

'I shouldn't be a bit surprised, would you? Well, I shall have to reward them for such a kind deed. I wonder whether one of you would come over tonight after the sun has gone down and water the bed for me? I don't expect the fairies will come now I'm back, do you?'

That evening the children took their old leaky watering-can next door and went to water the round bed. Mr. Reed watched them from the window. Ruth and David saw something by the bed – and what do you think it was?

There was a fine new wheelbarrow, and inside it were two strong spades and a perfectly splendid new red watering-can. There was a note inside the barrow too, that said: 'A present for the kind fairies who gave me such a nice surprise.'

The children didn't know *what* to do. Did Mr. Reed really think it was the fairies that had worked so hard? Oh, what lovely garden tools these were – just what they needed so badly. They stood and looked at them.

'How do you like your new tools?' shouted Mr. Reed from his window.

'Oh, are they for *us*?' cried the children in delight. 'It says in the note that they are for the good fairies.'

'Well, didn't you act like good fairies?' said the old man, smiling. 'You gave me a wonderful surprise, and now I'm giving you one. You did a very kind deed to a cross, bad-tempered old man. But I'm better now, and so is my temper, especially since I've had such a lovely surprise. So I hope you will often come to tea with me and play with the new puppy I have bought. Now water my garden and then take your things home to show your mother.'

'Oh, thank you *so* much,' said the children, so excited that they could hardly hold the watering-can properly. Whatever would mother say when she heard what had happened?

Mother was delighted.

'You deserve your surprise,' she said. 'You were kind to someone you didn't very much like, and now you have made a friend and had a lovely present.'

You should see David and Ruth gardening now with all their new tools. They are as happy as can be – and all because Ruth had a good idea and was kind to a cross old man.

THE NEWSPAPER DOG

Once upon a time there was a little dog called Tips. He belonged to Mrs. Brown who lived in Primrose Cottage at the end of Cherry Village.

He was a useful little dog. He guarded the house each night for Mrs. Brown. He kept her company when she was alone. He barked at any tramp who came up the front path – and once each week he fetched a newspaper for her from old Mr. Jonathan who lived all by himself in a little house on the hillside.

Mr. Jonathan bought the newspaper himself, and read it. Then he lent it to Mrs. Jones, and after that she passed it on to someone else. She couldn't often find time to go to fetch the paper herself, so Tips fetched it for her.

He started off each Thursday evening, ran all the way down the village street, went over the bridge that crossed the stream and up the hillside to Mr. Jonathan's cottage. He jumped up at the door and pushed it open. Then in he would trot and look for Mr. Jonathan.

The old man always had the paper ready for him, neatly folded up with a piece of string round it. He put the packet into Tips's mouth and off the little dog would go, running all the way home again, not stopping for anything until he reached Primrose Cottage and could drop the paper at Mrs. Jones's feet.

One day Mr. Jonathan thought he would do some spring-cleaning. So he called on Mrs. Jones and asked her to lend him her ladder.

'Dear me, what do you want to go climbing about on ladders for?' asked Mrs. Jones in surprise. 'You'll fall off, Mr. Jonathan, and hurt yourself.'

'Indeed I shan't!' said the old man. 'I'm going to paint my ceiling white, Mrs. Jones.

It is very dirty. So lend me your step-ladder, there's a good soul.'

'It's in the shed,' said Mrs. Jones. 'You can have it if you want it. But do pray be careful, Mr. Jonathan, for it's not a very steady pair of steps.'

Mr. Jonathan found the ladder and took it home. He mixed some whitening and started to do his ceiling. It looked lovely! All day he worked at it, and then went to bed.

He began again next day, whistling to himself, sloshing about on the ceiling with the whitewash, quite enjoying himself. And then a dreadful thing happened.

The postman dropped some letters in the letterbox and gave such a loud rat-a-tat that the shock made old Mr. Jonathan fall off his ladder. Down he went – and when he tried to get up he found that he couldn't.

'Oh dear, oh dear, I must have sprained my ankle, or broken my leg, or something,' the old man groaned. 'Whatever shall I do? Nobody else will come today, and I can't send anyone for the doctor. I have no neighbours to call to. I am all alone!'

He lay there on the floor, groaning. He really didn't know what he was going to do. Perhaps he would have to stay there all night long. If only somebody would come! But there was nobody to come at all.

And then, just as he was thinking that, Mr. Jonathan heard the sound of pitter-pattering feet, and someone came running up the front path. Then a little body hurled itself against the door which opened at once. It was Tips, the little newspaper dog, come to get his mistress's paper, for it was Thursday evening!

He saw Mr. Jonathan lying on the floor, and he was puzzled. He ran up to him and licked his hand. Then he sat down with his head on one side and said 'Woof!'

That was his way of saying: 'What's the matter? Can I help you?'

'I wish you could, Tips,' said Mr. Jonathan. And then he suddenly looked more cheerful. Perhaps Tips *could* help him. He looked round. The newspaper was on a chair, already tied up with string for Mrs. Jones.

'There's the paper, Tips,' said Mr. Jonathan, pointing. 'Fetch it here!'

Tips saw the paper, and took it into his mouth. He was just going to run off with it when Mr. Jonathan called him back.

'Don't go yet, Tips,' he said. 'Bring the paper here.'

The clever little dog understood. He ran over to Mr. Jonathan with the paper in his mouth. Mr. Jonathan took a pencil from his

pocket and wrote in large letters across the top of the paper:

'Mrs. Jones. I have fallen off the ladder. Please fetch the doctor. Mr. Jonathan.'

Then he pushed the paper once more into Tips's mouth and patted the waiting dog. 'Go home now,' he said.

Tips ran off, puzzling his little head to know why Mr. Jonathan was on the floor. He ran to his mistress as soon as he reached Primrose Cottage and dropped the paper at her feet. She picked it up, and caught sight of the message scribbled on the top.

'Good gracious me!' she cried. 'Poor old Mr. Jonathan! He's tumbled off the ladder!'

She ran for the doctor at once, and he took her along to Mr. Jonathan's in his car. It wasn't long before they had him safely in bed, his leg bandaged up, and a nice hot drink beside him.

'It was my clever little dog Tips who found Mr. Jonathan when he came for my weekly paper this evening,' said Mrs. Jones proudly to the doctor. 'Mr. Jonathan wrote a message on the paper, and, of course, I saw it when

Tips dropped the paper at my feet.'

Mr. Jonathan soon got well, and one morning Mrs. Jones and Tips met him going shopping for the first time, leaning on a stick.

'Now wherever are you going?' cried Mrs. Jones. 'I'm sure there's no shopping so important that I can't do it for you. Whatever is it you must buy, Mr. Jonathan?'

'It's something very special,' said Mr. Jonathan with a smile, and he went into a little shop nearby beckoning Tips and Mrs. Jones in too. And what do you suppose the special bit of shopping was? Why, a fine red collar for Tips!

'That's to show everyone what a clever, helpful little chap he is,' said Mr. Jonathan, putting it round the little dog's neck. 'He really does deserve it.'

I think so, too, don't you?

MR. CANDLE'S COCO-NUT

Mr. Candle was very proud of himself. He had been to the Fair in Oak-Tree Village, and had won a coco-nut at the coco-nut shy. He had paid a penny to the man there, who had given him four balls to throw at the coco-nuts.

The first ball didn't go near any coco-nuts at all. It was a very bad shot. The second ball nearly touched the nut in the middle. The third ball went wrong somehow, and knocked off the hat of a man quite a long way away. After Mr. Candle had said he was really very, very sorry, he took up his fourth and last ball, and threw that.

And, dear me, nobody was more surprised than he was to see it hit the very largest coco-nut of all and send it rolling to the ground! Mr. Candle was simply delighted. He picked it up and took it home with him. All the way home he was making a fine plan.

He would give a Coco-nut Party. That would be a most unusual party. He would give his guests cocoa to drink, because that *sounded* as if it ought to go with coco-nut to eat. He would have a big coco-nut cake, some coco-nut ice candy and he would cut up the piece of coco-nut left and hand round the bits for his guests to nibble. Yes, it would be a very fine Coco-nut Party indeed.

So Mr. Candle sent out his invitations. One went to Squiddle the Pixie. One went to Mrs. Popoff the Balloon Woman, and the third one went to Mr. Crinkle who painted wonderful pictures on the pavement outside the post office.

Mr. Candle made his coco-nut cake. It was a beautiful one with coco-nut in it and grated coco-cut sprinkled on top. Then he made the coco-nut ice candy – some in pink and some in white. It tasted lovely because Mr. Candle had a bit to see.

There was just over half the coco-nut left when Mr. Candle had finished. So he cut this up very neatly into nice little squares, and put them on a plate on the wide window-ledge ready for when his guests came that afternoon.

When they came Mr. Candle was ready to greet them, dressed up in his best green and red suit, with his new pointed shoes.

'Welcome to the Coco-nut Party!' he said. 'I am so pleased to see you. The party is because I won a coco-nut at the Fair.'

'How clever of you!' said Squiddle the Pixie.

'You *must* be a good shot!' said Mr. Crinkle.

'Splendid, Mr. Candle!' said Mrs. Popoff, beaming all over her kind red face.

Mr. Candle was so pleased. He thought what nice people his friends were. Down they sat to the coco-nut cake, the mugs of hot, sweet cocoa, and the coco-nut ice laid out on a blue dish. The pieces of coco-nut on the window-ledge were to be eaten after tea, when they were all playing games. It would be nice to have something to nibble at then, Mr. Candle thought.

They finished all the coco-nut cake because it was so good, and they ate all the coco-nut ice candy too. They drank every drop of their sweet cocoa, and then they wanted to play games.

'Let's play Hunt-the-Thimble!' said Mrs. Popoff, who simply loved that game. 'Mr. Crinkle, you hide the thimble – here it is – and we'll all go out of the room while you do it.'

Out they went and shut the door. Mr. Crinkle was a long time hiding the thimble. He simply could *not* think of a good place. But at last he put it on the head of a little china monkey on the mantel-piece. It looked just like a hat, and Mr. Crinkle felt sure nobody would notice it was a thimble.

He called the others in, and they began to hunt. Mr. Candle saw the thimble first and he sat down at once to show the others that he had seen it. He thought it would be a good idea to offer his friends a piece of the cut-up coco-nut on the window-ledge as soon as they had found the thimble too.

He got up to get the plate – and my goodness me, whatever do you think? There were hardly any pieces left! Somebody had taken them!

Who could it be? It must be Mr. Crinkle. He had been a long, long time hiding the thimble when all the others were outside the door. Mr. Candle was cross and upset.

'Did you eat my pieces of coco-nut?' he suddenly said to Mr. Crinkle. 'There's hardly any left. You must have eaten them when you were supposed to be hiding the thimble.'

Mr. Crinkle went very red.

'No, I didn't, Mr. Candle,' he said, in a

very hurt voice. 'I don't eat other people's bits of coco-nut unless they offer them to me. I hope I know my manners. I shan't stay and play with you any more. I shall go home.'

He put on his little red hat and walked out of the door. The others watched him go. Mr. Candle felt very worried.

'He *must* have eaten the pieces of coco-nut,' said Squiddle the Pixie. 'He was the only one alone in the room.'

Suddenly there was a little noise at the window. Squiddle, Mr. Candle and Mrs. Popoff all turned round quickly. And what do you think they saw? I'll give you three guesses!

They saw three little birds there, blue-tits,

44

dressed in pretty blue and yellow feathers –
and they all picked up a piece of the white
coco-nut and flew off out of the window in
delight; for tits, as you know, love nuts,
especially coco-nuts. I expect you have often
hung up a coco-nut for them and watched
them swinging upside down on it, pecking
away as hard as they can.

'It's the tits!' cried Mr. Candle. 'Look! The
naughty little birds! They've taken away three
more bits! They must have taken the other
pieces too, but I expect Mr. Crinkle was so
busy trying to think of a good place to hide the
thimble that he didn't notice the naughty
little robbers.'

'I haven't found the thimble *yet*,' said Mrs.

Popoff, looking all round.

'How dreadful to tell Crinkle he had eaten the coco-nut when he hadn't!' said Squiddle the Pixie, looking worried. 'He was really very hurt about it.'

'I'll call him back and say I'm sorry,' said Mr. Candle, shutting the window so that the blue-tits couldn't come in again. He ran to the door and looked up the street.

'Hie, Crinkle!' he shouted. 'Crinkle! Come back! You didn't eat the coco-nut – and we know who did.'

Mr. Crinkle walked back, still looking rather cross and upset.

'It was the blue-tits who ate that coco-nut,' explained Mr. Candle, taking his friend by the arm. 'Do forgive us for being horrid, Crinkle. There's just one piece left and you shall have that.'

Mr. Crinkle was a very good-natured little fellow, and he at once forgave Mr. Candle and the others for saying he had done something he hadn't. He ate the last piece of coco-nut, and then said: 'What about a game of Blind Man's Buff?'

So they all played at Blind Man and had a lovely time together. And when they said good-bye Mr. Crinkle said: 'I think a story ought to be written about how the blue-tits came and stole your coco-nut pieces, Mr. Candle. Then it would warn people not to leave them near the window, if the blue-tits are about. Don't you think so?'

Mr. Candle *did* think so – and that is why he told me to write this story!

CHIPPERDEE'S SCENT

Once upon a time the Queen of Fairyland emptied her big scent-bottle, and asked the King for some new scent.

'I don't want any I've ever had before,' she said. 'Get me something strange and lovely, something quite different from anything I've ever had.'

So the King sent out his messengers all over the place – to the topmost clouds and to the lowest caves, begging anyone who knew of a strange and lovely scent to bring it to the Queen. For reward he would give a palace set on a sunny hill, and twelve hardworking pixies to keep it beautiful.

Palaces were hard to get in those days, so anyone who had a lovely scent in bottle or jar journeyed to the Queen with it. But she didn't like any of them. She was really very hard to please.

Now there lived in a cave at the foot of a mountain a clever little pixie called Chipper-dee. He spent all his days in making sweet perfumes, and he made them from the strangest things. And just about this time he finished making the strangest and loveliest perfume he had ever thought of.

He had taken twenty drops of clearest dew and imprisoned in them a beam of sunlight and a little starlight. He had taken the smell of the earth after rain and by his magic he had squeezed that into the bottle too. Then he had climbed up a rainbow and cut out a big piece of it. He heated this over a candle-flame and when it melted he let it drop into this bottle.

Then he asked a two-year-old baby to breathe her sweet breath into the full bottle – and lo and behold, the perfume was made! It smelt glorious – deep, delicious, and so sweet

that whoever smelt it had to close his eyes for joy.

Now although he lived in a cave, the smell of this new perfume rose through the air and everyone who lived near smelt it. An old wizard sniffed it and thought: 'Aha! That is the scent that would please the Queen mightily! I will go and seek it.'

So off he went and soon arrived at the cave where Chipperdee sat working.

'Let me buy some of that new perfume of yours to take to the Queen,' said the wizard.

'No,' said Chipperdee. 'I am going to take it myself. I shall get a palace for it and twelve hard-working servants.'

'What do you want with a palace?' asked the wizard. 'Why not let me give you a sack of gold for that bottle of scent? The Queen may not like it at all – and you will still have the sack of gold! I will not ask for it back.'

'You know perfectly well that the Queen will love this new perfume,' said Chipperdee. 'Go away, wizard. I don't like you, and you won't get any scent from me! I start tomorrow to journey to the Queen.'

The wizard scowled all over his ugly face and went away. But he made up his mind to follow Chipperdee and steal the scent from him if he could. So when he saw the pixie starting off, he made himself invisible and followed him closely all day long.

Chipperdee felt quite sure that he was being followed. He kept looking round but he could see no one at all. But he could hear someone breathing! It was very strange.

'It must be that wizard,' he thought to himself. 'He's made himself invisible. He's going to steal my bottle of scent when I sleep under a hedge tonight. Ho ho! *I'll* teach him to steal it!'

When it was dark the pixie found a nice sheltered dell. He felt all around until he

found some little flowers with their heads almost hidden under heart-shaped leaves. He took out his bottle in the darkness, and emptied a little of the scent into each flower, whispering to them to hold it safely for him.

Then he filled the bottle with dew and set it beside him, curling up to go to sleep beneath a bush. He pretended to snore loudly, and almost at once he heard a rustling noise beside him, and felt a hand searching about his clothes.

The hand found the bottle and then Chipperdee heard quick footsteps going away. He sat up and grinned. Ho ho! The wizard thought he had got a fine bottle of scent – but all he had was a bottle of plain dew!

The pixie lay down again and slept soundly. In the morning he woke up, and looked round at the little flowers near him. They were small purple flowers, so shy that they hid their heads beneath their leaves. The pixie jumped up and picked a bunch. He smelt them. Ah! His scent was in the flowers now, and it was really wonderful.

Off he went to the court, and there he saw the wizard just presenting the Queen with the bottle of plain dew that he had stolen from the pixie. How Chipperdee laughed when the Queen threw it to the ground and scolded the wizard for playing what she thought was a stupid trick on her!

The pixie stepped forward and told the Queen how the wizard had followed him and tried to steal his rare perfume. 'But, Your Majesty,' he said, 'I poured the scent into these little purple flowers, and if you will smell them, you will know whether or not you like the scent I have made.'

The Queen smelt the flowers – and when she sniffed up that deep, sweet, delicious scent she closed her eyes in joy.

'Yes!' she cried. 'I will have this scent for mine! Can you make me some, Chipperdee? Oh, you shall certainly have a palace set on a sunny hill and twelve hard-working servants to keep it for you! This is the loveliest perfume I have ever known.'

Chipperdee danced all the way back to his cave and there he made six bottles of the strange and lovely scent for the Queen. The King built him his palace on a sunny hill, and he went to live there with a little wife, and twelve hard-working servants to keep everything clean and shining.

But that isn't quite the end of the story – no, there is a little more to tell. *We* can smell Chipperdee's scent in the early springtime, for the little purple flowers he emptied his bottle into still smell of his rare and lovely perfume. Do you know what they are? Guess! Yes – violets! That's why they smell so beautiful – because Chipperdee once upon a time emptied the Queen's scent into their little purple hearts!

THE QUARRELSOME TIN SOLDIERS

Once upon a time there lived on a low wooden shelf two boxes of soldiers. One army was dressed in green and the other in red. The green army had horses to ride on, brown, black and white, but the red army had none. They carried guns, and the green horse-soldiers carried swords.

All the soldiers belonged to Kenneth. He liked them very much and often took them out to play games with him. He had a fine wooden fort, and he loved making his toy soldiers march up and down the draw-bridge, and stand looking over the parapet of the fort.

The soldiers were very quarrelsome. The green horsemen hated the red foot-soldiers, and the red soldiers jeered at the green ones.

'You've only got stupid little swords,' said the captain of the red army to the green captain. 'We have fine guns. *You* wouldn't be much use against an enemy!'

'Ho, wouldn't we, then!' cried the green captain in a temper. 'Well, let me tell you this – *we* ride horses. *You* have to walk everywhere.'

'We don't mind that,' said the red captain, stoutly. 'We like marching. Anyway, it's silly to have horses you can't get off. You're stuck on to your horses, and even if you wanted to march you couldn't!'

Every night the two armies quarrelled and one night there was a battle. The teddy-bear and the golliwog did their best to stop the fight, but it wasn't a bit of good.

'You'll only end in being broken to bits,' said the golliwog. 'Then what will be the use of you? Kenneth won't want to play with you any more.'

'Hold your tongue, you stupid golliwog!'

said the green captain, galloping over the golliwog's toes and making him yell. 'Now, men, follow me! We'll go to the toy fort and we won't let the red soldiers in. We'll keep them out and show them what poor fellows they are.'

All the horsemen followed their captain, and the green army galloped over the floor to the gay wooden fort. It was painted red and yellow and had four wooden towers and a draw-bridge. Over the bridge galloped the soldiers and, as soon as they were in, one of them pulled up the draw-bridge by its little chain. Now no one else could get into the fort, except by climbing up the walls.

The red soldiers had no horses so they could not go so fast as the green army. But they made haste and marched at top speed across the floor to the fort. By the time they reached it the green horse-soldiers were all in their places, looking over the top of the parapet, or cantering up and down the yard in the middle of the fort, shouting orders and feeling very important.

The red captain lined his men up in a row

in front of the fort and told them to fire. Pop!
Pop! Pop! The little guns went off and tiny
bullets like seeds flew over the walls of the fort.
Some of the green soldiers were hit and little
holes were made in their tin uniforms.

They were very much upset. They shouted
with rage, and galloped about, making quite
a noise on the wooden floors of the fort. Then
suddenly the green captain ordered the draw-
bridge to be let down and commanded six of
his men to ride out and make a surprise
attack on the enemy soldiers outside.

The red soldiers were so astonished that

some of them were ridden down before they knew what was happening. One of them had an arm broken off and another one had his leg twisted the wrong way round. A third one lost his fine helmet, and cried bitterly because he couldn't find it.

'Courage, my men!' said the captain of the red soldiers when the green men had ridden back to the fort again. 'I am going to get the little cannon out of the nursery toy cupboard. With that we can shell down the walls of

the fort, and rush in to attack the enemy.'

But the toy cannon was too heavy for the little tin soldiers to drag along. It shot peas, so it could have knocked over a great many of the green soldiers in the fort.

'Well, never mind if it's too heavy,' said the red captain. 'Look, we'll use a battering-ram instead. Here's one that will do.'

The battering-ram was really a big hoop-stick of Kenneth's. Seven soldiers picked it up

and carried it to the fort. Then twelve red soldiers took hold of it, six on each side, and waited for their captain's word.

'Charge!' he cried, and fired off his little gun, making the golliwog nearly jump out of his skin, for he and the bear were almost asleep.

'Just look at those soldiers!' said the golliwog, sitting up. 'The reds are breaking down one of the walls of the fort. Wouldn't Kenneth be cross if he knew!'

'Don't you think we ought to wake him?' said the bear anxiously. 'I think he would be very sorry if the tin soldiers killed one another. He would never be able to play with them again.'

'Let's go and wake him,' said the golliwog. So without telling the soldiers the two stole out of the day nursery into the night nursery, where Kenneth slept.

Bang! Bang! Bang! The hoop-stick battering-ram crashed against the wooden wall of the fort, and inside the green soldiers galloped about in a panic. What would they do if the wall gave way?

It did! It suddenly came away from the

nails that held it and fell right down in the fort, knocking over two of the green soldiers as it fell. Then in poured the red soldiers, shouting in victory, shooting with their guns as they came.

The green soldiers soon pulled themselves together and they galloped at the enemy, slashing about with their swords, and that was how Kenneth found them when he came into the nursery with Golly and Teddy. He stood and stared in astonishment at his toy soldiers fighting one another so fiercely, slashing and shooting and yelling.

'How dare you behave like this!' he said suddenly. 'You will end in being broken to bits, and I didn't buy you to fight one another. I bought you to play with! Go back to your boxes and tomorrow I will come and talk to you.'

The soldiers had stopped fighting as soon as they heard Kenneth's voice. They were frightened. They trooped out of the wooden fort and went silently back to their boxes – all but seven of them who were so battered that they couldn't march or gallop.

The next day Kenneth lifted up the lids and looked at his toy soldiers. What a sight they were! Not one of them was whole.

'You're not fit to play soldiers with,' he said. '*You* haven't any arms – and *you* have only one leg – and *you* haven't a helmet – and *you* have a horse that has lost its head. What a dreadful sight you all are! I don't want you for soldiers any more. I shall have you for something else.'

So he took three of them for his railway station and made them porters. Four more he put on his toy farm to look after the hens and the sheep. Five of them he put to live in the dolls' house, and one of them had to drive the little toy motor-car. The others he thought would do to act in his toy theatre. Then he threw the cardboard boxes into the waste-paper basket, emptied out his money-box and went out of the nursery.

He bought a great big box of cowboys, some with horses and some without. How the soldiers envied them when they saw Kenneth playing games with them!

'You shouldn't have been so quarrelsome!'

said the golliwog. 'It's your own fault that you're stuck away in the farm and the dolls' house, instead of being proper soldiers.'

'We wish we could have another chance!' said the red and the green soldiers, looking longingly at the cowboys prancing about the floor on their big horses. But it wasn't any use wishing. They never did have another chance!

THE TALL PINK VASE

Jill and Leslie lived in one of two cottages. The cottages were joined on to one another. One was called Buttercup Cottage and the other was called Daisy Cottage. Jill and Leslie lived in Buttercup Cottage, but Daisy Cottage was empty.

Then one day a furniture van arrived outside Daisy Cottage. The children were very much excited. Hurrah! Someone was coming to live in Daisy Cottage at last!

'I wonder what the people will be like,' said Jill. 'I do hope there will be some children.'

But what a disappointment! There were no children at all. Only a plump little lady with merry, twinkling eyes called Miss Bustle.

'Bother!' said Jill, 'I wish there had been a boy or a girl too.'

'Look at that dreadful pink vase going in,' said Leslie suddenly. 'Oh, Jill! Isn't it an ugly thing!'

Jill looked. It certainly was the ugliest vase she had ever seen. It was a bright pink, very tall and narrow, and had big yellow flowers here and there.

Jill's mother loved flowers and had many lovely vases – green jars, blue bowls and yellow jugs, which the children loved. They had never seen such an ugly thing as the pink vase going into the cottage next door.

'I don't think we shall like that person much if her things are all like that dreadful vase,' said Jill. 'I expect she will have paper flowers instead of real ones, and a china dog instead of a real puppy.'

'And mats that mustn't be dirtied, and cushions you mustn't lean against,' said Leslie. 'I don't think we'll make friends with our new neighbour, Jill.'

'Children, children!' called mother. 'It's not polite to stare like that. Come away from the wall and play in the garden at the back.'

The children didn't bother any more about Miss Bustle. They went to school, played in the garden, went for walks and took no notice of the cottage next door at all. If they had, they would have seen that Miss Bustle was simply longing to smile at them and talk to them. But they ran by Daisy Cottage without a single look.

Then one day Leslie happened to look at Daisy Cottage from their back garden and he saw the dreadful pink vase standing at one of the windows.

'Oh, Jill, look! There's that ugly vase again!' he cried.

'Well, I *shan't* look,' said Jill. 'It was quite bad enough the first time. Come on, Leslie, let's play cricket with your new ball.'

'You can bat first,' said Leslie. 'I'll bowl.'

He bowled his new ball to Jill. She missed it and it went into the rose-bed. She found it and sent it back to Leslie. He bowled again.

It was an easy ball. Jill lifted her bat and swiped at it. Crack! She sent the ball right up

into the air, spinning over the wall next door in the direction of the upstairs windows. The children watched it in fright. Would it break a window?

No – it struck the tall pink vase that stood at an open window and broke it in half! Crash! The pieces fell down inside the window. The cricket-ball rolled along the window-ledge and fell outside the window down to the flower-bed below.

The children looked at one another in dismay. Whatever would Miss Bustle say? They waited for her to put her head out of the window – but nothing happened.

'Perhaps she's out,' said Leslie.

'Yes, I remember now – she is,' said Jill. 'I

saw her go out with a basket about half an hour ago.'

'Let's go and get our ball,' said Leslie. So they climbed quickly over the wall, found their ball and climbed back. They sat down on the grass and looked at one another.

They were both thinking the same thing. If Miss Bustle was out, perhaps they needn't own up to breaking the vase. She might think the curtain had blown against it and knocked it down.

'Do you think we need say anything?' asked Jill at last.

Leslie went red. 'We *needn't*,' he said. 'But

we must, Jill. We'd be cowards not to own up.'

'And, oh, dear, I expect Miss Bustle loves that vase better than anything in the world,' said Jill, with a groan. 'And we'll have to buy another out of our money-box.'

'Look, there she is, coming back,' said Leslie. 'Come on, Jill, let's get it over while we feel brave.'

So they went to the door of Daisy Cottage and knocked. Miss Bustle opened the door and stared at them in surprise.

'Please,' said Leslie, 'we've come to say we're very very sorry but our cricket-ball broke your pink vase and if you'll tell us how much it was we'll buy you another.'

'Broken that pink vase!' exclaimed Miss Bustle. 'Have you *really*?'

'I'm afraid so,' said Jill, very red in the face.

'Well, I *am* glad it's broken at last!' said Miss Bustle, in a delighted voice. 'An old friend gave it to me and I've always hated it, but I didn't like to throw it away as it was given to me. I've always hoped it would get broken, it was so very ugly, but somehow it never did. And now at last it's smashed. Oh, dear me, I *am* glad! Come in, do, and have a bun and some lemonade, and see my new puppy. I only brought him home today.'

Well, would you believe it! Jill and Leslie were so surprised and delighted to hear that Miss Bustle, instead of being angry with them, was really pleased! They could hardly believe their ears. They stepped inside and found that Daisy Cottage was the gayest, prettiest, cosiest little place they had ever seen.

She showed them the puppy in his basket and then went to get the lemonade and buns.

'Isn't it a pretty house?' said Jill to Leslie. 'Not a bit like we imagined. And isn't Miss Bustle nice?'

'You know,' said Miss Bustle, hurrying back with a jug, 'I didn't think you were very nice children. You never spoke to me or smiled. I thought you were horrid. But now I know better. It was so nice of you to come and own up about the vase, because it *might* have been one I liked. And I can see now that you are nice, bright, smiley children.'

Jill told Miss Bustle how they had seen the pink vase and hated it. 'We *were* silly!' she said. 'We thought you'd be like that vase, so we didn't bother about being good neighbours at all. Do forgive us.'

'Of course, of course,' said Miss Bustle, setting ginger buns in front of them. 'I'd forgive anyone anything if they had broken that horrid pink vase. Do come and see me often. I've got a nephew and niece coming to stay with me soon, so perhaps you would come out for picnics and motor rides with us?'

'Oh, *rather*!' said Jill and Leslie happily. 'Thank you very much!'

Now they are so much in Daisy Cottage with Miss Bustle and the puppy that their mother says she really thinks they ought to live there altogether!

'Wasn't it a good thing we owned up about that broken vase!' Jill often says to Leslie. 'We *should* have missed a lot of fun if we hadn't!'

WHISKERS AND THE PARROT

Whiskers the cat lived with Miss Nellie, and was her great pet. He had a special chair of his own with a special cushion, a china dish with kittens all round it, and a saucer of blue and yellow.

So you can guess that he thought a great deal of himself. The other cats he met out in the garden didn't like Whiskers at all. They thought he was selfish, proud and stuck-up.

'One day you'll have your punishment,' said Tailer, the next-door Tabby. But Whiskers yawned in his face very rudely and didn't even bother to answer.

And then Miss Nellie bought a parrot in a cage! Good gracious me, you should have seen Whiskers' face when he saw the parrot sitting in its cage in a sunny corner of the dining-room. The cage hung from a hook in the ceiling, and the parrot sat in the sun and fluffed out all her feathers.

She saw Whiskers and cocked her grey and red head on one side.

'Hallo, hallo, hallo!' she said.

Whiskers nearly shot out of the room with fright. What was this thing that looked like a big bird and talked like a human being?

'Woof, woof, woof!' said the parrot, pretending to bark like a dog.

Whiskers mewed in fright and ran under the table. He thought there really was a dog in the room.

'Ha-ha, ha-ha, ha-ha!' jeered the parrot. 'Hallo, hallo! Pretty Polly, pretty Polly!'

Just then Miss Nellie came into the room and laughed to see Whiskers under the table.

'Why, Whiskers!' she cried. 'Surely you are not frightened of my Polly parrot? I want you to be friends.'

But that was just what Whiskers was not going to be! As soon as he was used to the parrot and knew that it was only a big bird that could talk, he made up his mind to catch Polly somehow. He would wait until Miss Nellie was safely out of the way and then he would get down that big cage and eat the parrot.

So he waited his time, and at last his chance came. Miss Nellie went out to tea with a friend and left her parrot and her cat shut up in the dining-room together.

'Miaow!' said Whiskers fiercely, looking up at the cage. 'Now I'm going to get you!'

'Pretty Polly, pretty Polly!' cried the parrot, climbing up and down her big cage. 'Hallo, hallo!'

Whiskers crouched to spring up at the cage. He leapt right up in the air and sprang on to the side of the cage. Crash – crash! The hook came out of the ceiling and the cage fell with a loud bang on to the floor!

Whiskers was frightened. He didn't know that his weight would bring the cage down. The parrot was frightened too. Whiskers ran into a corner to hide.

The parrot looked round – and saw that the

crash had made the door of the cage fly open.
Ha! Now she could get out and fly round a bit!

Out of the cage she hopped and flew up to
the top of the curtain. Whiskers watched her
in surprise. Perhaps he could get that parrot
now. He crept out from the corner and lay
watching, swishing his tail from side to side.
The parrot saw the moving tail and suddenly
flew down to the table. Before the surprised
cat knew what was happening the parrot shot
down and nipped his tail hard, right at the tip.

'Miaow!' cried the cat in pain and surprise.

'Ha-ha, ha-ha!' laughed the parrot, sitting
on the top of the clock. Whiskers leapt at the
big bird, who at once spread her wings and
flew to the electric light over the table,

screeching loudly as she went. Then it was the parrot's turn. She suddenly flew at Whiskers and pecked him on the nose!

'Miaow!' wailed the cat, and the parrot flew up to the top of a picture, where she screeched and squawked very happily.

Whiskers wondered what to do. Then he thought of a good idea. He would creep into the parrot's cage and lie down there. Perhaps when it was dark the parrot would go back to her cage again and then Whiskers could get her! So as soon as the parrot's back was turned, Whiskers crept into the cage. Polly was happily pulling all the flowers out of a vase and took no notice of Whiskers at all.

Then she looked round to see where the cat was, and when she spied him in the cage how she laughed! In a trice the parrot flew down and shut the door of the cage with a clang. Whiskers was a prisoner!

'Ha-ha, ha-ha!' chuckled the mischievous parrot in glee, and settled down on Whiskers' own cushion, in Whiskers' own chair. Soon Whiskers saw that the parrot was pulling all the fluff out of the cushion!

Whiskers mewed angrily and tried to get out of the cage – but the door was fast shut. Whiskers clawed at the door, but it was no good. He could *not* open it!

And there Miss Nellie found him when she arrived home again. The first thing she saw when she switched on the light was the parrot fast asleep on the curtain-rod. Then she saw the cage on the floor, and to her great surprise, spied Whiskers inside, with the door fast shut!

'O-ho, Whiskers!' she cried. 'So you jumped at the cage and made it fall down, did you? And Polly escaped out of the cage and you got in! And somehow or other the door was shut and made you a prisoner! Well, it serves you right. I shall leave you there for the night, and then, perhaps, you won't even *look* at the parrot-cage again.'

So there poor Whiskers had to stay all night long, and Polly laughed and chuckled, screeched and squawked whenever she thought of him.

The next day the cage was opened and Whiskers crawled out. He ran into the garden, and found that all the cats there had heard what had happened – and how they teased him!

'You won't be so proud now, Whiskers!' they said. 'Who got caught in the parrot-cage? Ho-ho!'

And now Whiskers never takes any notice

of the parrot at all, and would never dream of eating it – but Polly hasn't forgotten. She cries: 'Poor pussy, poor pussy!' whenever she sees Whiskers – and he doesn't like it at all!

THE ODD LITTLE BIRD

Once upon a time there was a fine fat hen who was sitting on twelve eggs. Eleven of the eggs were brown but the twelfth was a funny greeny-grey colour. The hen didn't like it very much. She thought it must be a bad egg.

'Still,' she thought to herself, 'I'll see if it hatches out with the others. If it doesn't, well, it will show it is a bad egg.'

After many days the hen was sure her eggs were going to hatch.

'I can hear a little 'cheep cheep' in one of them!' she clucked excitedly to all the other hens. Sure enough one of the eggs cracked, and out came a fluffy yellow chick, who cuddled up in the mother-hen's feathers with a cheep of joy.

Then one by one all the other eggs cracked too, and tiny fluffy birds crept out – all except the greeny-grey egg. No chick came from that. It lay there in the nest unhatched.

'Well, I'll give it another day or two,' said the hen, sitting down on it again. 'After that I won't sit on it any more.'

In two days the hen found that the twelfth egg was cracking too. Out came a small bird – but it wasn't a bit like the other chicks!

It was yellow, certainly – but its beak was bigger and quite different. Its body was different too, and the little creature waddled

about clumsily instead of running with the others.

The mother hen didn't like it. She pecked it and clucked: 'Oh, you funny-looking little thing! I'm sure you don't belong to me.'

The other chicks didn't like the little waddling bird, either. They called it names and shooed it away when it went to feed with them. It was sad and unhappy, for not even the mother-hen welcomed it or called it to enjoy a tit-bit as she did the others.

'I'm the odd one,' it said to itself. 'I wonder

why? I can't run fast like the others, and I don't look like them either. I am ugly and nobody wants me.'

The odd little bird grew faster than the others, and at last it was so much bigger that the little chicks didn't like to peck it any more, for they were afraid it might peck back and hurt them. So they left it alone, and stopped calling it names.

But the mother-hen was not afraid of it. She was often very cross with it indeed, especially when the rain came and made puddles all over the hen-run.

For then the odd little bird would cheep

with delight and go splashing through the puddles in joy.

'You naughty, dirty little creature!' clucked the mother-hen. 'Come back at once. No chicken likes its feet to be wet. You must be mad, you naughty little thing!'

Then the odd little bird would be well pecked by the hen, and would sit all by itself in a corner, watching the rain come down and wishing it could go out in it.

One day it found a hole in the hen-run and crept through it. Not far off it saw a piece of water, and on it were some lovely white birds, swimming about and making loud quacking noises. Something in the odd little bird's heart cried: 'Oh, if only I could be with those lovely birds, how happy I should be!'

But then it grew sad. 'No,' it said to itself, 'I am a queer, odd little bird. Nobody wants me. But all the same I will just go to the edge of the water and paddle my feet in it. I can run away if those big white birds chase me.'

So off it went and paddled in the water. It was lovely. At first the big white ducks took no notice of the little bird, and then two came swimming up quite near to him.

'Hallo!' they cried. 'What a little beauty you are! Come along with us and have a swim. We'd be proud to have you.'

At first the little bird didn't know that the ducks were talking to him. But when he saw that they really were, he was too astonished to answer. At last he found his voice, and said: 'But, lovely creatures, surely you don't want me, such an odd, ugly little bird as I am!'

'You're not odd or ugly,' cried the ducks. 'You are a beautiful little duck, like us. Come along, it is time you learnt to swim. Don't go back to those funny little chicks any more. Live with us, and have a fine swim on the water!'

The odd little bird could hardly believe what he heard. So he wasn't odd or ugly, after all! He was only different from the chicks because he was a duckling! And he would grow up to be like these lovely white creatures, and swim with them on the water. Oh, what happiness!

'Quack, quack!' he said, for the first time,

and swam boldly out to join the ducks. The old mother-hen spied him through the hole in the run and squawked to him to come back. But he waggled his tail and laughed.

'No, no!' he cried. 'You will never make a hen of me. I'm a duck, a duck, a duck!'

THE MECCANO MOTOR-CAR

Tom had made a meccano motor-car to put Elizabeth's dolls in. It was rather a queer-looking car, but when Elizabeth had put in a few little cushions out of her dolls' house, and sat her dolls in the seat, it looked quite real.

'We shall have to push it along the floor because it won't go like a real car,' said Tom. 'Wait a minute though! Where's my clockwork engine? I know how to take the clockwork out of that, and perhaps I can put it into the meccano motor-car.'

He tried it – and it worked! He wound up

his home-made motor-car and it ran along the floor by itself, taking the dolls with it. Tom and Elizabeth were delighted.

They showed it to Mummy when she came to put them to bed.

'It's very good,' she said. 'Leave it there on the floor, and I'll show it to Daddy when he comes in.'

So they left it there, with all the dolls sitting on the seats. And that night, when everyone was asleep, you should have seen how excited those dolls were! They came alive and called to the sailor doll to wind up the meccano motor-car to let it take them round and round the nursery again.

'I say!' said the curly-haired doll suddenly, 'Let's call the pixies in! They're holding a party under the lilac bush tonight, and they would so love to see our car.'

So they called to the pixies, and they all came tumbling in at the window in great excitement.

'Let's have a ride, let's have a ride!' they cried, when they saw the motor-car. In they got, and one of the dolls showed them how to

steer the little wheel. The pixies soon learnt
how to drive, and my goodness me! how they
tore about the nursery, almost running over
the pink rabbit and nearly knocking down the
blue teddy-bear.

They made such a noise that Tom and
Elizabeth woke up. They slept in the room
next to the nursery, and they sat up in bed and
wondered whatever was happening.

'It sounds as if something was tearing about
across the nursery floor,' said Tom. 'Whatever
can it be?'

'Let's go and look!' said Elizabeth. So they
crept out of bed and went to the day-nursery.
The moon was shining right into it and they
could see everything quite clearly.

And weren't they surprised! They saw their

toy motor-car tearing round and round, full of small pixies who were yelling with excitement. The dolls all stood watching, and the blue teddy-bear held up his paw, saying: 'Sh! Sh! Sh! Not so much noise! You'll wake the children!'

Tom and Elizabeth could hardly believe their eyes. They stood peeping in at the door, watching. And as they watched they saw the meccano motor-car dash straight into a chair. Bump! It turned over and all the pixies fell out.

'Oh, my goodness!' cried Elizabeth, quite forgetting that she didn't mean to be seen.

As soon as she had cried out, all the pixies gave a squeal of fright and flew out of the window. The toys rushed back to the cupboard and sat themselves down at once, keeping as still as could be. The meccano motor-car didn't move. It lay on its side.

Tom and Elizabeth were just going to step into the nursery when they heard their mother's voice.

'Elizabeth! Tom! Whatever are you doing? Go back to bed at once!'

'But, Mummy, such funny things have been happening in the nursery,' said Tom. 'We saw some fairies riding in the motor-car we made, and all the toys were alive!'

'Oh, nonsense! You were just dreaming,' said Mummy. 'Go back to bed before you get a cold, both of you!'

So to bed they had to go, and they soon fell asleep again. In the morning they looked at one another.

'*Did* we really see those fairies and our toys all alive?' said Elizabeth. 'Or did we dream it?'

'Well, we couldn't *both* have dreamed it, could we?' said Tom. 'We'll see if the motor-car is still lying on its side in the nursery.'

It was! And do you know, tucked in one of the seats was a tiny silver wand with a shiny

star on the end of it! One of the pixies must have left it behind.

'There!' said Elizabeth, in delight. 'It *was* real. We didn't dream it. Oh Tom! Let's use the wand and wish a wish!'

So when they are in bed tonight, they are going to wave that tiny wand and wish a wish. I do wonder what will happen!

THE JUMPING FROG

All the toys in the nursery were perfectly happy before the horrid jumping frog came. They used to play peacefully together, having a lovely time, never quarrelling, never snapping at one another or teasing.

But as soon as the jumping frog came he spoilt everything. For one thing he talked all the time, and for another thing he was always jumping out at the toys and giving them frights.

They couldn't bear him, but they were too polite to say so. They begged him not to frighten them, but he took no notice.

'You don't need to be frightened of *me*!' he

would say. 'It's only my fun.'

But it wasn't fun to the toys. The teddy-bear fell over and bumped his nose when the frog jumped out at him from behind the cupboard; and the captain of the wooden soldiers broke his gun through tumbling down in fright when the frog jumped right on top of him.

'One of these days,' said the big humming-top solemnly to the frog, 'one of these days frog, you will be sorry for all these tricks of yours. People who frighten others always end in getting a terrible fright themselves. And when that happens, *we* shan't help you!'

One night the jumping frog planned to frighten the golliwog. The frog could wind himself up, so he was able to jump about whenever he wanted to. He knew that the golliwog often walked round by the window at night so he thought he would hide behind the big waste-paper basket and jump out at him as he came walking by. How frightened the golliwog would be! How he would squeak! How fast he would run, and how the jumping frog would laugh!

The frog wound himself up and hid behind

the waste-paper basket. He waited and he waited. At last he peeped out. Ah, was that the black golliwog coming? Yes, it must be. Now for a good high jump to frighten him out of his skin!

The frog jumped – but oh, my goodness me! it wasn't the black golliwog after all. It was the big black kitchen cat! The jumping frog saw him just as he landed flat on the cat's back.

'Sssssssssss-tt!' hissed the cat angrily, and flashed round to see what it was that had fallen on her back, and was now slipping to the floor. Out went her paw and gave the jumping frog a good smack. He leapt away in fright. The cat went after him.

All the toys peeped out of the cupboard in surprise. Whatever was happening?

'It's the frog!' cried the golliwog. 'He jumped out at the cat, thinking it was me, I expect. And now the cat is chasing him! Oh my, what a fright he is in.'

'Serve him right!' cried the toys.

'Help! Help!' squealed the frog, jumping for all he was worth.

But the toys were far too much afraid of the cat to go to his rescue. Each of them felt that the frog was getting what he deserved, and what he had so often given others – a good fright!

Jump! Jump! Jump! The frog leapt high in the air half a dozen times as the cat went after

him. He was so frightened that he didn't look where he was going and once he nearly jumped right into the fire.

The toys watched, their eyes wide open in surprise. Whatever would happen?

Suddenly the cat shot its claws out at the frog and something clattered to the floor. It was the frog's key, which the cat had clawed out of his back. The frog jumped higher still, frightened almost out of his life. He was near the waste-paper basket, and to the toys' enormous surprise he jumped right into it!

He hadn't meant to – but there he was, at the bottom of the basket, among Nurse's bits of cotton and torn-up paper. And just at that very moment his clockwork ran down. He could jump no more. He couldn't wind himself up, either, because his key had fallen out. There he must stay.

The cat didn't know where the frog had gone. She hunted about for a while and then ran out of the nursery to catch mice in the kitchen. The toys ran to the waste-paper basket and peeped in.

'Help me out,' said the frog. 'I've had such a fright.'

'Serve you right!' said the golliwog sternly. 'We can't help you out, the basket is too tall. You'll be emptied into the dust-bin tomorrow, and that will be the end of you. You've always been fond of giving other people frights, so you can't complain of what has happened to *you*!'

The next morning the housemaid took the

waste-paper basket downstairs, and emptied it into the dust-bin. The jumping frog went in all among the tea-leaves and potato-peel. He was very unhappy, and wished many times that he had been kind and jolly, instead of unkind and mean.

'I wonder what happened to him in the dust-bin,' said the toys to one another. But no one ever knew!

THE LITTLE BROWN PONY

Monty had a little brown pony for his birth-day. It was a pretty little thing, not very tall, with a long brown mane and tail.

Monty wasn't very pleased. 'Pooh!' he said to himself when he saw it. 'Why didn't Dad give me a horse? I don't want a silly little pony! It won't be able to gallop nearly fast enough for me. I'd like a big horse that goes like the wind.'

He didn't say all this to his father, though. No, he didn't dare! His father called Monty to him and spoke gravely to him.

'Now listen, Monty,' he said. 'You are a very lucky boy to have a pony for your birthday, and I want you to be sure to treat it kindly and well. You are not very good with animals, for you let your rabbit die, and you never remembered to take your puppy for a walk when you had one. The gardener will teach you how to look after your pony properly, and you may ride him twice a day, if you wish. And remember, always be kind to him!'

Monty promised, but after a little while he grew bored with having to brush his pony and see to its water and food. He found that it

couldn't go fast enough for him and soon he began to slash it and shout at it. The little thing was frightened and did its best for Monty, but he was impatient and unkind.

The small girl who lived next door to Monty often used to watch him riding the pony. She had always wanted a pony of her own, but her Daddy couldn't afford one. So she watched Monty's pony instead, and sometimes she would climb over the wall and go to help the gardener groom the pretty little animal.

'Do you like doing that sort of work?' asked Monty scornfully one day, watching Ann brush his pony till its coat gleamed and shone.

'Yes, I do,' said Ann. 'I wish I could do it always. I love your little pony, Monty.'

'Well, look here – if you'll look after my pony for me, I'll let your ride it once a week,' said Monty. 'I hate looking after it. It's a silly animal, anyway. I want a great big horse that will gallop!'

Ann promised to care for his pony each day, and once a week Monty let her have a short ride on it. Ann grew very fond of the pony, and the fonder she grew the more she hated seeing Monty whip the little animal and shout at it.

'You shouldn't do that,' she said to him. 'It's unkind.'

'Hold your tongue!' said Monty rudely. 'Whose pony is this, yours or mine? I shall do what I like with it!'

The pony grew frightened of Monty and one day when the boy galloped it round and round the field, slashing it with a big stick, the pony lost its temper. It stood quite still and wouldn't move a step. Ann was watching over the wall, and she shouted to Monty to jump off.

'Stop it, Monty!' she called. 'The pony is getting angry.'

'What do I care!' cried Monty, and he hit the pony hard. It suddenly galloped off, nearly throwing Monty, and rushed for the open gate that led into the road. Ann saw that it was running away with Monty. In a trice she was over the wall, and reached the gate just as the pony got there. She caught hold of the reins and dragged at them with all her strength.

The pony stopped just outside the gate, and Monty slid off. Ann's arms were almost pulled out of her shoulders.

'You're a cruel boy!' she said, through her tears. 'You don't deserve to be saved when the

pony's running away. I wish *I* had him! I'd love him and be kind to him. You don't like him a bit. You don't even look after him. I do all that!'

'What's all this?' said a deep voice, and who should look over the hedge at the other side of the road but Monty's father. 'Ann, I saw what you did. You're a brave little girl, and I'm proud of you. As for Monty, I'm thoroughly ashamed of him. I saw him lashing the pony and I don't wonder it ran away.'

Monty's father led the pony back to its stable and there he heard from the gardener how Ann looked after it each day, and how all that Monty did was to ride it and whip it every day. Monty's father looked very stern. 'Very well,' he said to Monty. 'You have disobeyed me. Now you must be punished. As Ann loves the pony and looks after it so well, she shall have it for her own. You don't deserve to go riding at all, and you are never to ride the pony again. It's Ann's now.'

Well, what do you think of that? Ann was so overjoyed that she could hardly say a word. Monty turned red and ran off. The pony gave a little whinny of delight and snuggled its nose into the small girl's hand.

'I'm happy now!' whinnied the pony.

'So am I!' cried Ann. 'We'll have *lovely* times together!' They do, too – you should just see them galloping round the field on a sunny morning! As for Monty, he always looks the other way.

ENID BLYTON is Dragon's bestselling author. Her books have sold millions of copies throughout the world and have delighted children of many nations. Here is a list of her books available in Dragon Books:

FIRST TERM AT MALORY TOWERS	35p	☐
SECOND FORM AT MALORY TOWERS	35p	☐
THIRD YEAR AT MALORY TOWERS	35p	☐
UPPER FOURTH AT MALORY TOWERS	35p	☐
IN THE FIFTH AT MALORY TOWERS	30p	☐
LAST TERM AT MALORY TOWERS	35p	☐
MALORY TOWERS GIFT SET	£2.25	☐
6 Books by ENID BLYTON		
THE TWINS AT ST. CLARE'S	35p	☐
SUMMER TERM AT ST. CLARE'S	35p	☐
SECOND FORM AT ST. CLARE'S	35p	☐
CLAUDINE AT ST. CLARE'S	35p	☐
FIFTH FORMERS AT ST. CLARE'S	35p	☐
THE O'SULLIVAN TWINS	35p	☐
ST. CLARE'S GIFT SET	£2.25	☐
5 Books by ENID BLYTON		
MYSTERY OF THE BANSHEE TOWERS	35p	☐
MYSTERY OF THE BURNT COTTAGE	30p	☐
MYSTERY OF THE DISAPPEARING CAT	30p	☐
MYSTERY OF THE HIDDEN HOUSE	30p	☐
MYSTERY OF HOLLY LANE	35p	☐
MYSTERY OF THE INVISIBLE THIEF	30p	☐
MYSTERY OF THE MISSING MAN	30p	☐
MYSTERY OF THE MISSING NECKLACE	30p	☐
MYSTERY OF THE PANTOMIME CAT	30p	☐
MYSTERY OF THE SECRET ROOM	30p	☐
MYSTERY OF THE SPITEFUL LETTERS	30p	☐
MYSTERY OF THE STRANGE BUNDLE	30p	☐
MYSTERY OF THE STRANGE MESSAGES	30p	☐
MYSTERY OF TALLY-HO COTTAGE	30p	☐
MYSTERY OF THE VANISHED PRINCE	30p	☐
CHILDREN'S LIFE OF CHRIST	30p	☐
THE BOY WHO TURNED INTO AN ENGINE	30p	☐
THE BOOK OF NAUGHTY CHILDREN	20p	☐
A SECOND BOOK OF NAUGHTY CHILDREN	35p	☐

TEN-MINUTE TALES	20p ☐
TWENTY-MINUTE TALES	20p ☐
MORE TWENTY-MINUTE TALES	30p ☐
THE LAND OF FAR-BEYOND	20p ☐
BILLY-BOB TALES	20p ☐
TALES OF BETSY MAY	20p ☐
NAUGHTY AMELIA JANE	30p ☐
AMELIA JANE AGAIN	20p ☐
BIMBO AND TOPSY	30p ☐
EIGHT O'CLOCK TALES	20p ☐
THE YELLOW STORY BOOK	20p ☐
THE RED STORY BOOK	20p ☐
THE BLUE STORY BOOK	20p ☐
THE GREEN STORY BOOK	20p ☐
TRICKY THE GOBLIN	20p ☐
THE ADVENTURES OF BINKLE AND FLIP	30p ☐
THE ADVENTURES OF MR. PINK-WHISTLE	20p ☐
MR. PINK-WHISTLE INTERFERES	30p ☐
MR. PINK-WHISTLE'S PARTY	20p ☐
MERRY MR. MEDDLE	20p ☐
MR. MEDDLE'S MUDDLES	20p ☐
MR. MEDDLES MISCHIEF	30p ☐
DON'T BE SILLY MR. TWIDDLE	20p ☐
ADVENTURES OF THE WISHING CHAIR	30p ☐

All these books are available at your local bookshop or newsagent, or can be ordered direct from the publisher. Just tick the titles you want and fill in the form below.

Name ...... Emma MargritBliss.

Address ...... 23 hillcroft ave Pihne

...... Middsex Northhar...

Write to Dragon Cash Sales, PO Box 11, Falmouth, Cornwall TR10 9EN

Please enclose remittance to the value of the cover price plus:

UK: 18p for the first book plus 8p per copy for each additional book ordered to a maximum charge of 66p

BFPO and EIRE: 18p for the first book plus 8p per copy for the next 6 books, thereafter 3p per book

OVERSEAS: 20p for first book and 10p for each additional book

Granada Publishing reserve the right to show new retail prices on covers, which may differ from those previously advertised in the text or elsewhere.